MARGRET & H.A. REY'S

Curious George's

First Day of School

WALKER BOOKS

AND SUBSIDIARIES

LONDON · BOSTON · SYDNEY · AUCKLAND

First published in Great Britain 2008 by Walker Books Ltd
87 Vauxhall Walk, London SE11 5HJ

This edition published 2018

2 4 6 8 10 9 7 5 3 1

This book has been typeset in Gill Sans MT Schoolbook.
Illustrated in the style of H. A. Rey by Anna Grossnickle Hines

Printed in China

British Library Cataloguing in Publication Data:
a catalogue record for this book is available from the British Library

ISBN: 978-1-4063-8889-3

www.walker.co.uk

This is George.

He was a good little monkey and always very curious.

Today George was so excited, he could barely eat his breakfast.

"You have a big day ahead of you, George," said his friend, the man

with the yellow hat.

It *was* a big day for George. It was the first day of school and he had
been invited to be a special helper.

George and his friend walked together to the schoolyard. Some of the
children were nervous, but George could not wait for the fun to begin.

In the classroom George's friend introduced him to Mr Apple.

"Thank you for inviting George to school today," the man

with the yellow hat said to the teacher. Then he waved goodbye.

"Have a good day, George. I'll be back to pick you up after school."

The children were excited to have a monkey in class. "George is going to be our special helper," Mr Apple told them.

And what a helper he was!
At storytime George held
the book.

At maths time the
children could count
on George.

And at recess George made sure everone

had a ball . . .

and a well-balanced snack.

8

After lunch Mr Apple got out paints and brushes. George saw red, yellow and blue paint. Three colours were not very many. George was curious. Could he help make more colours?

First George mixed red and blue to make . . .

purple.

Next George mixed red and yellow to make . . .

orange.

Then George mixed
yellow and blue to make . . .

green.

Finally George mixed all
the colours to make . . .

. . . a big mess!

The children thought the mess was funny. But Mr Apple did not.

"Oh, dear," he said. "We are going to need something to clean this up. Everyone please sit quietly while I look."

George did not mean to make such a mess and he certainly did not want to sit quietly. He wanted to help — it was his job, after all. George had an idea.

14

In the

hallway

George

found

a closet.

In the

closet

he found

a bucket.

In the bucket

he found just

what he needed . . .

15

A mop!

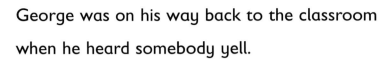

George was on his way back to the classroom
when he heard somebody yell.
"Stop! Stop! What are you doing with my
mop?" The janitor ran after George.
"Stop! Stop! No running in the halls!" The principal
ran after the janitor.

But George was going too fast to
stop. He grabbed the doorway and
swung inside, and . . .

S P L O S H !

The bucket tipped,
the mop dropped,
and George slid
across the floor.

18

Now the mess was even bigger.

Mr Apple looked surprised. The principal frowned. The janitor just shook his head.

And George – poor George. He felt terrible. Maybe he was not such a good helper after all.

The children felt terrible too. They did not like to see George looking so sad. They thought he was a great helper. Now they wanted to help him.

So the children all lent a hand (and some feet).

And before anyone knew it, the mess was gone!

"That little monkey sure is helpful," the janitor said.

"It looks like Mr Apple has a whole class full of helpers,"
the principal added.

At the end of the day, when George's friend arrived to pick him up, Mr Apple said, "Thank you for all of your help, George. We hope you will come help us again." The children cheered. They hoped George would come again too.

George waved goodbye to his new friends. What a great day it had been! He could not wait to come back to school.